Flying Pig
to the Rescue

Other books by Judy Corbalis

The Wrestling Princess
Oskar and the Ice Pick
Your Dad's a Monkey
Porcellus the Flying Pig

JUDY CORBALIS

Flying Pig
to the Rescue

Illustrated by David Parkins

KNIGHT BOOKS
Hodder and Stoughton

First published in Great Britain in 1991 by Hodder and Stoughton

Knight Books edition 1993

Printed and bound in Great Britain for Hodder and Stoughton Children's Books, a division of Hodder and Stoughton Ltd., Mill Road, Dunton Green, Sevenoaks, Kent TN13 2YA (Editorial Office: 47 Bedford Square, London WC1B 3DP) by Clays Ltd., St Ives plc.

British Library C.I.P.

Corbalis, Judy
  Flying pig to the rescue.
  I. Title
  823[J]

ISBN 0 340 57741 X

Chapter 1

The most famous space styion in the world swept across the screen. Seated at the controls of the satellite, the astroporcs waved to the viewers at home as they sped out of Earth's atmosphere and into deepest space.

Clustered round the television set, their snouts pressed to the screen, Porcellus and his brothers and sisters watched in awe.

'It's the fastest satellite ever built,' said their father.

'And the cleverest,' said their mother. 'What did Professor Einstyn say it could do?'

'Tell the time! Predict the weather! Examine the stars! Study sunspots! Keep planes on course! Give out recipes! Wake up porkers in the morning! Help with homework! Find lost piglets!' shouted the piglets.

'Right,' said their father. 'And any pig who needs help with any problem can dial the satellite and get an answer.'

'From here it looks just like a speck in the sky,' said Porcine, the smallest piglette. 'You'd never think it was so clever.'

The satellite was still racing into outer space. 'Have you got your cello ready, Porcellus?' asked his mother. 'It's your lesson tomorrow.' Porcellus pulled a face. 'I'll do it later,' he said. 'I'm too busy watching now.'

'Don't forget,' said his mother.

Suddenly, the television screen went blank and a message appeared.

EMERGENCY!
DO NOT ADJUST YOUR SETS.
THE SPACE STYTION IS OUT OF
CONTROL AND THE ASTROPORCS
ARE NOT MAKING CONTACT
WITH EARTH. WE SHALL
RESUME TRANSMISSION AS
SOON AS POSSIBLE.

Porcine slipped her trotter into Porcellus's. 'You know what I think?' she whispered.

He nodded. 'They may need help from the Flying Pig,' he whispered back.

Chapter 2

Professor Alboart Einstyn

The night before, warmly wrapped in their blue coats, yellow hats and red gloves, the piglets had piled into the pigmobile for a trip to Hogrell Bank Observatory.

'I hope you're going to behave yourselves,' said their mother, Hogmanay. 'Professor Einstyn's a very old friend of ours.'

'You're very lucky piglets,' said their father, QMP. 'And mind you ask sensible questions. Alboart Einstyn's one of the cleverest porkers in the world. He designed the space stytion.'

The pigmobile drew up in front of a large locked iron gate and QMP handed a pass to the guard who let them drive through. Hogrell Bank Observatory sat on a hill: it had a domed top and the roof opened up for a huge telescope to slide out into the sky. An elderly boar with long white bristles, a white coat and spectacles, came up to meet them. ·

'QMP! Hogmanay!' he said. 'I'm so pleased you've come!'

'So are we, Alboart,' said QMP. 'And this is our litter.'

'Delighted to meet you,' said Einstyn. 'I expect you want to see the spacecraft.'

'Yes, please,' said the piglets.

'This way, then,' said Einstyn, leading them into a large room. In front of a bank of television screens sat boars and sows busy at computers. They looked up as the piglets trooped in. Porcellus noticed several of them staring at the large lumps on his back. He went red and felt embarrassed and tried to hide them by pushing in among his brothers and sisters. 'Ouch. Your back bumps are digging into me,' complained Sowphie.

'Don't be mean,' said Porcine. 'Porcellus can't help his bumps. It's not his fault.'

The professor moved over to the television sets. 'Our space styion is the cleverest piece of electronic computer equipment in the entire world,' he said. 'Watch.' He flicked a switch and the numbers and patterns on the bank of screens changed into pictures.

'Goodness! We're looking right inside the satellite,' said Hogmanay. 'Can they see us?'

'Certainly,' said Einstyn. He clipped a microphone onto his coat. 'Calling D.A.S. Calling D.A.S.'

'What's D.A.S.?' asked Porcine.

'It's short for Dial A Satellite,' said one of the pignicians.

The astroporcs, a hog and a sow, turned towards them and waved.

'My young friends want to say hello,' said the professor.

The piglets shouted and waved back.

'Look now,' said Einstyn. He switched on a huge overhead screen and a picture of Earth appeared.

'This is how Earth looks from the space stytion,' he explained.

'Really?' asked one of the piglets.

'Yes,' said the astrosow from the screen.

Everybody jumped. 'Can they hear what we're saying?' they cried.

'Only if they tune in to us,' said a pignician. 'Mostly they're very busy gathering information.'

'How long will they have to stay up there?' asked Porcellus.

'You'll see through the telescope, it's a space stytion in two sections,' said Einstyn. 'The front half's a satellite and once they've set up all the data banks and equipment, they'll re-enter Earth's atmosphere in that front section, leaving the back section up there working in the sky.'

Lights winked on and off across the screens.

'Those are porkers from all over the world phoning in,' said a pignician. 'So far we've handled three million calls.'

'Incredible,' said QMP.

The observatory telescope was enormous and much more powerful than QMP's telescope in their back yard. When it was Porcellus's turn to look, he couldn't believe his eyes. The satellite was huge, not a tiny speck at all. One after another the piglets took turns. Porcine, being the runt of the litter, was very very small and had to be lifted up to the eyepiece by Professor Einstyn. 'It's so big it makes me feel even smaller still,' she said.

'Time to leave, now,' said QMP.

The piglets thanked the professor. 'From tomorrow,' he told them, 'you'll be able to see the astroporcs on television if you tune in to the special channel.'

'Will they be able to see us?'

'No,' said Einstyn. 'And you'll only be able to see small areas inside the satellite. Nothing like here. But you can come back again for another visit, if you'd like to.'

'Yes, *please*,' everyone had cried, piling into the pigmobile for the ride home.

So today, after school, they had raced to turn on the television. The astroporcs had been taking photographs of the universe and relaying them back to the observatory. A number showed how many calls had been made to Dial A Satellite.

'Fourteen million,' Sowphie had said. 'Gosh.'

Up until now the space styion had seemed perfectly all right. 'I don't understand it,' thought Porcellus.

'The picture's coming back,' cried one of his brothers. 'Look.'

Professor Einstyn appeared on the screen. 'We have lost all radio contact with D.A.S.,' he announced. 'We're working on the problem now but the spacecraft has no link back to Earth. Fortunately our television monitor is still receiving pictures. Please stay tuned for further information.'

'But why has this happened, Professor?' asked the television commentator. 'What's gone wrong?'

The professor looked grave. 'I'm afraid we have no idea,' he said. 'We're completely baffled at this stage.'

Porcellus looked at Porcine. 'This is definitely a case for the Flying Pig,' he whispered.

Chapter 3

On screen, the astroporcs desperately pulled at the satellite controls, trying to clear the communications system. 'Are you there, Professor Einstyn?' called the astrosow. 'Are you receiving us?' But there was no answer.

Hogmanay looked grave. 'They don't realise we can still see them' she said.

'Poor astroporcs,' said one of the piglets. 'They must know they'll never come back alive.'

'Will they starve to death?' asked another.

'Not for a long time,' said QMP. 'They'll probably go mad or the space styion may collide with a meteorite. At present they're heading out of our solar system towards the Hamdromeda Galaxy. I've just phoned Alboart at the observatory. He wants me to go over right away.'

'Can we come too?' cried the piglets.

'As long as you're good,' said QMP.

'But *why* has it suddenly happened?' whispered Porcellus to Porcine who was sitting next to him in the pigmobile. 'It's very odd.'

'Can you help them?' whispered Porcine.

'I hope so,' he said. 'But I don't know how. I'll have to try to find out more at the observatory.'

'You'd better find some way of slipping off as well,' said Porcine. 'I'll cover up for you here.'

Porcellus squeezed her trotter.

'I've brought the two-way radio,' she whispered 'It's in my coat pocket.'

'Thanks,' said Porcellus.

Einstyn was waiting for them at Hogrell Bank. 'This a terrible business,' he said. 'We're at our wits' en

None of my calculations is working. It's as if some colossal force is pulling the satellite away into space yet there's nothing there.'

'What can you do?' asked QMP.

'Nothing,' said Einstyn. 'Astroporconomy is no help now. The most brilliant porkers in the world are all working on the problem but so far . . . nothing.'

They sat down in the darkened room in front of the bank of screens. Einstyn pointed to the astrohog who was doing calculations on an abacus. 'The power supply to the maths computer has failed, too,' he said. 'And I'm afraid that because of the speed they're travelling . . .'

He broke off as the screens went dark. Pignicians came running in. 'Professor,' cried one, 'come quickly! We're losing sight of the satellite.

'This is your chance,' whispered Porcine to Porcellus, thrusting his radio into his trotter. 'Hurry, climb up the telescope and out onto the roof.'

'But someone'll see me,' said Porcellus.

'I'll make sure they don't. Go on! Hurry.' She gave him a push.

Porcellus slipped along the wall and and crept into the next room. Behind him, he heard Porcine give a shrill squeal. 'Look! Quick, everybody. There's something on this screen here!'

Everyone rushed to see what was happening and Porcellus seized his chance. He clambered up onto the telescope's shiny surface, crawled along to the end then raised himself up very carefully.

He was standing right out in the sky. The roof was too far away from the telescope for him to be able to reach it or to jump onto it and the ground below was miles away. 'It's no use. I'll break my neck if I slip,' he thought and he was about to slide back inside again when, without any warning, he felt an odd prickling in his back bumps, gooseflesh broke out over his hide and a bright light began to shine all round him. Looking down, he saw he was covered with glowing stars: an extra-large one glittered on his chest. His hide tingled and his trotters shook. From his back bumps there slowly unfolded two beautiful multi-coloured wings. He breathed in deeply, his wings fluttered, then moved more strongly and he was airborne. He was the Flying Pig once more!

Chapter 4

As Porcellus swooped and soared, enjoying the wonderful feeling of flying again, he heard a shout from the observatory behind him. 'What's that? Something's streaking through the sky over there.'

He dived low down behind the shelter of some trees. 'The astroporcs,' he thought. 'I must try to help them.'

But the night was so clear and starry that he had trouble locating the spacecraft among all the pinpoints of light. His father had said it was heading towards the Hamdromeda Galaxy. He found the constellation of Pigasus and the Great and Little Boar, then he scanned the sky again to find the moving blip of the satellite. Summoning up his superspeed, he flew towards it as fast as he could.

He seemed to be slowing down. The farther he flew, the thinner the air became and the harder it was to breathe. 'I *must* at least tell them we're trying to help them,' he panted, chasing the space stytion as it raced on. Making one final effort, he flapped his wings furiously and drew level with the capsule. At the portholes, he could see the faces of the terrified astroporcs as he swept by the glass.

'Try to hang on. We're sending help!' he shouted.

'Save us!' called the astroporcs.

And as Porcellus, faint and dizzy from his marathon flight, headed back to Earth, he thought he heard a mocking hiss from the sky behind him, 'Help? Save them? Nothing can help them now.'

As he flew lower, Porcellus's strength began to return. Using his super-sight, he located the observatory. He wondered if anyone had discovered he was missing and how Porcine had covered up for him. She was the only one of his family who knew he was the famous Flying Pig. He could go straight to Professor Einstyn and offer to help but he didn't have any plan to suggest. It would better to go back and talk to Porcine first.

He was careful to fly low over Piggsville to keep below the range of the telescope. Circling Hogrell Bank, he made out the pigmobile below him but to his horror, as he was about to land, out came his father, Einstyn and the other piglets. Porcellus did not dare call Porcine on the radio. One of the others might hear. He landed behind a tree and hid, watching as his father counted heads. 'Twelve, thirteen . . .' he grunted. 'One of you children has been left behind. Who is it?'

'He'll know it's me missing in a minute,' thought Porcellus and his heart sank. Just at that moment, he saw Porcine look up at the sky, then deliberately slip over. 'Ow!' she screamed. 'My trotter. Oh! Ouch! I think I've broken it. Help, someone please.'

As everyone clustered round her, Porcellus peeped out from behind the tree. His wings began to quiver and wobble and shrank out of sight, his stars disappeared and he was back in his ordinary clothes again. He crept over to the group round his sister.

'You're being nothing but a nuisance tonight, Porcine,' said QMP. 'Your trotter's perfectly all right. Now line up in order of height again so I can check who's missing. One, two, three . . . That's odd. There are fourteen here. I must have miscounted.'

Porcine grinned at Porcellus. 'Just in time,' she whispered.

'But the astroporcs are still in danger,' thought Porcellus. 'As soon as we're back, I'll talk to Porcine. We've got to save them.'

Hogmanay was waiting for them at the door of the sty. 'I'm afraid you haven't heard the latest bulletin,' she said. 'It was on the news a few minutes ago. The satellite's orbit has changed again.'

'Excellent,' said QMP.

'No, not excellent at all,' said Hogmanay. 'It's swung back towards Earth, heading straight for Piggsville. And when it crashes, it won't just destroy our sty and the observatory but everything for hundreds of miles around.'

Chapter 5

By the next morning, terrified porkers were creating chaos everywhere. All the roads out of Piggsville were jammed with families trying to escape. 'You'd better not go to school today,' said Hogmanay.

'The schools are shut, my dear,' said QMP. 'It was on the news.'

Porcellus was pleased. This would make it easier for him to get away.

'You can all do schoolwork here this morning,' said QMP. 'And in the afternoon you can either run around in the yard or play backgammon indoors.'

'Porcellus promised to help me with my Herd Studies project,' said Porcine. 'We can work on that today. It's my special study. I have to find out about Swilliam Swillberforce and the slave pigs of Africa.'

'That sounds interesting,' said QMP.

'Could they work in your study?' asked Hogmanay. 'It's quieter.'

'Certainly, my dear,' said QMP.

'You're brilliant,' said Porcellus as they closed the study door behind them.

'I know,' said Porcine. 'But you've still got to get away from here without anyone noticing.'

'I'll slip out through the wallow window,' said Porcellus, 'but you'll have to pretend you're talking to me if Mother comes past.'

Porcine sighed. '*And* I have to study all day. I'd much rather be with you. But we've got to help the astroporcs. The Flying Pig's their only hope now.'

'I'll do what I can,' said Porcellus. 'But the farther I go in space, the slower I'm flying. And I still haven't found out what's pulling them out of orbit.' He paused. 'I know it sounds silly but I thought I heard a voice laughing as I flew back.'

'In space? What kind of a voice?' asked Porcine.

'I don't know exactly. Nasty. Sort of jeering,' said Porcellus. 'But I was very tired. I probably imagined it.'

'Hmm,' said Porcine. 'I wonder.'

Chapter 6

Outside the sty, Porcellus slipped into the secluded space behind the garage where no-one could see him. 'Oh I do wish I could fly,' he whispered. The prickling feeling in his bumps started up, he felt his wings uncurling and the stars began to glow all over him. 'I'll have to be careful not to be seen,' he thought as he flexed his wings and began to hover in the air. It was daylight so he couldn't see the space stytion but he remembered what his teacher had told them in school. 'The sun rises in the east and sets in the west.' His father was always saying the same thing. 'So if I fly west,' he thought, 'sooner or later, I'll get to the part of Earth where it's still dark and then I can spot the satellite.'

He decided it was safer to keep very high in the sky. Below him, the roads were crammed with cars and trucks and even tractors, as thousands of road-hogs tried to drive out of Piggsville. Police sirens were screaming everywhere as Pigg of the Yard and his porkers tried to control the traffic.

Farther and farther west he flew until Piggsville was out of sight and the sky became paler, then greyer and finally black as night, and stars began to appear. Searching the heavens, he spotted the satellite heading back towards Earth. 'If it carries on at this rate,' he calculated, 'it will crash in just two days' time. I haven't got long. I must act fast.'

Taking several very deep breaths, he soared up, towards the out-of-control craft. And as he did so, he noticed that a number of stars seemed to go out, just as if a lot of lights had been switched off. A whole area of the sky was totally dark, where a minute ago there had been hundreds of tiny winking stars.

Something was going wrong with the sky. 'Stars don't just suddenly stop shining like that,' said Porcellus aloud. 'Something's badly wrong.' And he sped even faster towards the darkness where the crippled satellite raced on, carrying its doomed astroporcs on a collision course with Earth.

Chapter 7

The air was getting thinner again but Porcellus was still flying strongly. The space stytion grew larger as he approached and the stars around it twinkled brightly. Suddenly, all those stars went out, too. 'What's happening?' wondered Porcellus. The satellite was still shining clearly as it hurtled to Earth and he was close enough now to see the astroporcs peering through the portholes. Still puzzling over what had happened to the stars, Porcellus swooped towards the spacecraft. And as he did so, something sticky grabbed his trotter and pulled him backwards. An evil voice came echoing towards him.

'Don't touch that satellite,' it hissed. 'That's mine.'

Porcellus turned his head and found himself staring into the glowing eyes of a hideous monster.

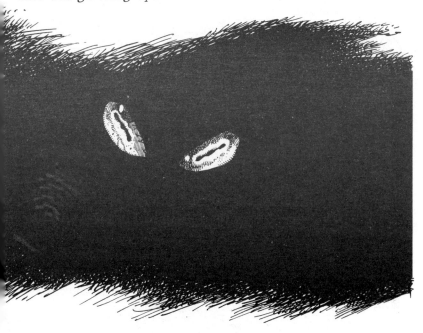

Chapter 8

Two cruel glittering red-gold eyes stared down at him. Porcellus flapped his wings wildly but was not strong enough to break free. 'Who are you?' he cried.

The huge eyes flickered. 'The Ozosaurus,' rumbled the monster.

'But where are you?' cried Porcellus. 'You're just two horrible eyes. You haven't got a body.'

An evil laugh rolled past him. 'Of course I've got a body,' hissed the Ozosaurus. 'But it's the same colour as the sky. You can't tell which is my body and which is not. I'm camouflaged.'

Porcellus peered with his super-vision and gradually made out the outlines of a huge slimy body. Its six long jellyfish-like legs with feelers on the ends splayed out across the sky. 'That's why the stars disappeared,' he said. '*You* covered them up.'

'Right,' growled the Ozosaurus.

Porcellus tried to shake his trotter free from the monster's grasp but it was stuck fast. His hide felt torn and sore. 'You can't get away from me,' snarled the Ozosaurus. 'And if you keep on trying, I'll rip every bit of hide off your trotter with my suckers. I want to talk to you. What are you doing here? Who sent you?'

'Nobody sent me,' said Porcellus boldly. 'I've come by myself to save the satellite. The space stytion's out of control. It's heading back to Earth and if it crashes, the astroporcs and thousands of other porkers will be smashed to pieces.'

'That's right,' said the Ozosaurus sliding its slimy feeler along Porcellus's trotter and tearing off more of his hide. 'Yes, with luck, that satellite will wipe out hundreds of pigs and a large piece of Earth's surface.'

'Luck?' said Porcellus. 'What do you mean, luck?'

'Lucky for me if it wipes out some of those horrible little beasts,' snarled the monster. Its eyes glittered nastily. 'Watch.'

It flicked up one of its jelly-fish legs and flipped the satellite slightly to one side. 'I control that spaceship,' it growled.

'*You*?' said Porcellus. 'Are you the one that's done this to the space styion?'

'Yes,' said the Ozosaurus proudly.

'But why?'

'I'm hungry,' rumbled the Ozosaurus. 'And I like to graze on my pastures when I'm hungry.'

'What do you mean?' said Porcellus.

'Without interference,' said the monster.

'What interference?' asked Porcellus. 'What are you talking about?'

'Stupid satellites,' snarled the monster. 'Space styions. Astroporcs prying around. And rude inter-fering rockets cluttering up my pastures. I can't graze in peace any more.'

'But where *are* your pastures?' asked Porcellus.

'Over there.' The Ozosaurus pointed with a feeler. It glared at Porcellus.

'But the satellite wasn't going anywhere near there,' said Porcellus. 'That's the Southern Cross with the South Pole below it.'

Two dark sparks shot out of the Ozosaurus's eyes. Porcellus's hide twitched with fright. His trotter stung and ached where the Ozosaurus was clutching it.

'I graze above the South Pole,' said the monster. 'And the North Pole, too. And I'm sick of all these nasty little space probes being sent out to check what I'm doing. If I'm hungry, I need to eat. And when I need to eat, sometimes I need to eat a lot. That's my business. Too bad for the Earth pigs.'

'But what do you graze *on*?' asked Porcellus.

'What do you think?' said the monster. 'Over there, that delicious patch. Can't you see it.'

'It's like a thick custard with a hole in it,' said Porcellus.

'That is a hole,' said the Ozosaurus. 'I was so hungry I ate through it there. Right through the ozone layer down into the sky.'

'The ozone layer?' cried Porcellus. '*That's* the ozone layer?'

'You're not very clever,' said the monster. 'Of course it's the ozone layer.'

Porcellus was amazed. 'And *you* made the holes in it?'

'Well, who else did you think it was?' said the Ozosaurus rudely. 'And I'm sick of nosey pigs trying to stop me.'

'But you can't do that,' said Porcellus. 'You're damaging the Earth.'

'So are all the Earth pigs,' said the Ozosaurus. 'Why shouldn't I?'

Porcellus had just opened his mouth to answer when his super-acute hearing picked up a faint cry from the satellite. The astroporcs! They were still racing towards Earth at breakneck speed.

He had a sudden idea. Bending over quickly, he sank his teeth into the feeler that was holding him. His mouth filled with bitter purple liquid which he spat out as fast as he could. The taste was disgusting. The monster gave a hideous scream, snatched back its feeler and Porcellus was free.

'I must get back to Earth and get help,' he thought as he wrenched away. And he sped off through the sky as fast as his wings could carry him. Behind him, he could hear the screams and threats of the furious monster. 'I'll destroy you,' it roared. 'You crazy, interfering little Flying Pig. You'll be sorry you did that. I'll tear you to pieces and scatter you across the sky.'

Chapter 9

The sky grew paler. As Porcellus flew down, down towards Earth, he tried to think of some way to save the astroporcs. Floating high above his own yard, he saw his brothers and sisters playing pig-in-the-middle below. He flew in a wide circle to the end of his street and dropped unnoticed into a tall tree. As he landed, he felt the familiar wobbling in his wings, his stars disappeared and he changed back to his normal piggy self. Scrambling down the trunk, he ran home and tapped on the study window.

'About time, too,' said Porcine. 'All the others are out playing and I'm stuck here with Swilliam Swillberforce. What happened?'

As Porcellus told her, she shook her head. 'There's no point in going to the observatory,' she said. 'No-one will believe you. And Professor Einstyn won't be able to see the monster even with that powerful telescope.'

'But I have to get back to the space stytion as soon as I can,' said Porcellus. 'The satellite's due to crash in thirty-six hours.'

'It's getting dark,' said Porcine. 'You'll need some sleep tonight to get your strength back.'

Porcellus realised he was very, very tired. He yawned.

'Your trotter's bleeding badly, too,' said Porcine. 'Better get some oinkment and a bandage on it before Mother sees it.'

Early next morning, while the other piglets were still asleep, Porcine crept into Porcellus's bed, woke him up and beckoned him outside. 'I have to talk to you,' she whispered. 'This afternoon you've got a cello lesson.'

'Yes,' said Porcellus. 'But I can't go. I've got to get back to the astroporcs.'

'You *must* go,' said Porcine. 'And as soon as the lesson's over, hide the cello somewhere and set off. It'll be getting dark by then.'

'But Mother will notice I'm missing.'

'I'll tell her you're staying to swill after your lesson,' said Porcine.

'But what can I do about the Ozosaurus?' said Porcellus. 'Even the Flying Pig's not strong enough to defeat it.'

Porcine thought for a while. 'I don't know if this'll work,' she said, 'but you did say its feelers were sticky.'

'They were,' said Porcellus. 'Look at my trotter. All the skin's torn off it.'

'I've got an idea,' said Porcine. 'I don't know if it'll work but . . .'

'It's worth a try,' said Porcellus, when she had finished.'

'If it doesn't work,' said Porcine gravely, 'then you . . .' She broke off.

'I know,' said Porcellus and he squeezed her trotter. 'I'd better get my cello and set off now. There's not much time left.'

'Don't forget your two-way radio,' said Porcine. 'I wish I could come too. I'll be really worried down here wondering what's happening.'

'I'd take you on my back,' said Porcellus, 'but the breathing's the problem. You couldn't stand the lack of oxygen.'

'It's all right,' said Porcine with a sigh. 'Someone ought to be down here in case you need help anyway.'

Chapter 10

Porcellus had been gone for over an hour before it began to get dark. 'Mother,' said Porcine, 'why don't we have swill early. Then afterwards, we can watch the satellite through our telescope in the garden!'

'What's going to happen,' asked one of the other piglets. 'Will we all be killed?'

'Of course not,' said Hogmanay in a worried voice. 'Don't be silly.'

'But it's going to crash on Piggsville,' said another piglet.

'Right near here,' said a third. 'It was on the television.'

Several piglets began to cry.

'It's not as bad as that,' said QMP. 'All the pignicians at the observatory are still working to save the satellite. I'm sure they'll come up with something.'

He turned to Porcine. 'That's a very good idea,' he said. 'We'll all take a look at it through our telescope after swill.'

And he went off to set things up.

He had only been outside for two or three minutes when they heard him calling, 'Quickly, all of you! Hurry! There's a U.F.O. in the sky above Piggsville. I can see it quite clearly.'

The piglets crowded round taking turns to look. 'It's

gold,' said Sowphie. 'And it's flying way out into space really fast.'

Porcine's heart sank. She put her eye to the telescope. It was Porcellus: she hadn't left enough time for him to get away safely.

'I must phone Einstyn immediately!' cried QMP. 'It may be a new star.'

Porcine crept into the sty behind him and waited while he telephoned. He put the receiver down looking very pleased. 'It's a U.F.O. all right, my dear,' he said to his wife. 'Alboart told me they're following it through their big telescope and with their tracking equipment. It seems to be heading for the doomed satellite.'

'The sky's gone mad' said Hogmanay. 'All sorts of crazy things are happening. But what's Alboart going to do about it?'

'That's the exciting thing,' said QMP. 'They're going to launch an emergency rocket to attack the U.F.O. and to try to deflect the satellite back on course. They think it's probably the U.F.O. that's caused all the trouble.'

'When are they launching the rocket?' asked Porcine in a small voice.

'In half an hour,' said her father. 'And if you don't mind, my dear, Alboart's invited me to watch the launch, so I'll drive over immediately.'

'Is it a very big rocket?' asked Porcine.

'Enormous,' said Q.Marcus cheerfully. 'Guaranteed to smash that U.F.O. completely to pieces.'

Chapter 11

Porcine slipped into the bed-pen and crawled under her hay duvet. 'Porcellus,' she called softly into her radio. 'Can you hear me?' There was silence for a moment then Porcellus's voice came crackling over.

'Just.'

'The observatory's going to launch a rocket at you,' whispered Porcine. 'They think you're making the satellite go out of orbit. They think you're a U.F.O.'

Porcellus was silent for a minute. 'The Flying Pig's very strong,' he said, 'but not strong enough to stand up to a rocket attack.'

'Listen carefully,' said Porcine. 'Father's going over to the observatory now. I'm going to hide in the back of the pigmobile under the blanket and when I get there, I'll do what I can to stop the rocket attack.'

'But Professor Einstyn will recognise you,' said Porcellus. 'He won't believe you. You told me the same thing.'

'I'll have to chance it,' said Porcine. 'I've got no choice. But I'll have to do it without Father seeing me.'

'You're very brave,' said Porcellus. 'Good luck.'

'Good luck, yourself,' said Porcine, turning off the radio.

She brushed her hide, smoothed out her dress and washed her trotters, then she slipped out through the wallow window and hid under the blanket on the back seat of the pigmobile, waiting for her father to come out.

Chapter 12

The pigmobile stopped at the gates of the observatory, then drove in. From under the blanket, Porcine heard her father greet one of the pignicians. 'Professor Einstyn can't leave the telescope,' said the pignician, 'so he sent me to fetch you. We'll be launching the rocket any moment now.'

Porcine had no time to lose. She didn't dare risk opening the door, so she rolled down the window just enough to squeeze out, and set off at a safe distance after QMP and the pignician. Slipping behind a bush, she picked up a rock and flung it hard towards the pigmobile. It hit the bonnet with a loud clunk.

'What on earth's that?' said the pignician, turning back. 'It sounded like your car.'

QMP swung round towards the noise and Porcine, seizing her chance, raced as fast as she could up to the large observatory door.

'I have to see Professor Einstyn right now,' she panted. 'It's urgent.'

'You can't come in here without a pass,' said the guard.

'It's about the U.F.O.,' said Porcine. 'Please.'

'Sorry,' said the guard. 'I'm under orders. It's more than my job's worth to let you in.'

From the corner of her eye, Porcine saw QMP and the pignician making their way back towards the observatory. 'I'll get a pass and come back tomorrow,' she said quickly. She peered at the sky. 'Look up there,' she said, 'I can see that U.F.O.' The guard craned his neck. 'Where?' he said. 'I can't see it. Are you sure?'

'Over there,' said Porcine. 'See. Right by the Pole Star.'

And as the guard stared upwards, Porcine slid noiselessly away round the side of the building.

The windows were far too high for her to reach and there were no more doors. 'But there must be some way in,' thought Porcine. The brick walls were solid without any chinks or gaps big enough for even a very small piglette. She searched around for any trees nearby that she could climb to reach window level but there were none. And then she saw something. The drainpipe.

The bottom of the pipe opened into a drain on the ground. If she crawled up the pipe, she could get to the storm gutter on the first floor, then crawl along the guttering under thc window, climb up over the sill and get inside. The pipe was narrow but Porcine was very small and although it would be a tight fit, she was sure she could manage it. She gave a little shiver at the thought of being in the dark in the pipe, then she thought of Porcellus and the astroporcs and boldly bent down, stuck her head into the opening and wriggled inside.

It was wet and smelly in the pipe and Porcine felt herself getting squeezed more and more tightly the higher she climbed. She began to feel panicked. What would happen if she got stuck? No-one would ever find her. It was pitch dark and her trotters kept slipping and grazing against the sides. Just as she was starting to think the pipe would never end, she saw a chink of light ahead, scrabbled towards it and pulled herself out into the storm gutter. She lay there panting for a minute. Her dress was covered with slime and mud and her hide was matted and dirty. From the nearby window shone a bright light and she could hear voices talking.

She crawled along until she was below the window and lifted her head cautiously to peer inside. Professor Einstyn was talking to a pignician. He seemed very worried and kept running his trotters through his long white bristles. QMP was nowhere to be seen but he was sure to arrive at any minute. Porcine tried the window. It was locked. She rapped hard on the glass and the two porkers looked up in astonishment. Einstyn came over to the window, opened it and lifted her inside. 'Good gracious,' he said. 'I do believe it's one of QMP's piglettes. Whatever are you doing outside my window?'

Chapter 13

Porcine heard her father's voice in the next room. 'I came to see you,' she said. 'Please. I've got to talk to you alone. It's terribly important. It's about the U.F.O. Please listen to me.'

Einstyn looked at her muddy dress and dirty hide. 'But how did you get up to the window sill?'

'I crawled up the drainpipe,' said Porcine. 'I had to tell you something top secret and the guard wouldn't let me in. But if Father finds out I'm here . . .'

'Up the drainpipe,' said Einstyn. 'You're very fearless and determined.'

'I must talk to you before you launch the rocket,' said Porcine desperately. 'Please, please just give me five minutes. But don't let Father or anyone else in.'

QMP's voice came closer. Einstyn looked thoughtful. 'Five minutes can't do any harm,' he said. 'And you certainly worked hard to get to see me.' He turned to the pignician. 'Ask Mr Porcus to wait next door for a few minutes please. And not a word about who's in here with me.'

The pignician nodded and Porcine's heart leapt with relief.

'And now,' said Einstyn, 'tell me what it is you think I ought to know.'

Porcine took a deep breath. 'You won't believe me,' she said, 'but I've just seen an extra-terrestrial.'

'An extra-terrestrial?' said Einstyn sharply. 'Are you sure?'

'Not exactly,' said Porcine, 'but I think it must have been. It was gold and covered with stars and it had large multi-coloured wings. And it spoke to me.'

'What did it say?'

'It told me it was going to try to rescue the

astroporcs.'

Einstyn leaned forward. 'And where did you see this extra-terrestrial?'

'Outside our sty in Piggsville,' said Porcine.

'Did anyone else see it?'

'No, I was all by myself when it spoke to me,' said Porcine.

'Gold with stars and multi-coloured wings, did you say?' said Einstyn. 'Hmm. I wonder.' He took her trotter. 'Come through this door,' he said. 'Don't worry. We won't meet your father.' And he led her into the room with the enormous telescope.

'Hmm,' he said, peering into it. 'Multi-coloured wings? That's interesting. And you say it was friendly?'

'Really friendly,' said Porcine. 'Oh, please don't send a rocket to smash it. At least wait and see if it can help the astroporcs. It was very kind to me.'

'It's certainly true that this U.F.O. has multi-coloured blurs along each side,' said the professor. He thought for a minute or two, then gazed through the telescope again. 'Perhaps we should wait,' he said to himself.

He looked hard at Porcine. 'I believe you,' he said. 'I won't launch our rocket tonight. We'll give this extra-terrestrial a chance. You've been very brave to bring me the information. Thank you. But how will you get home?'

'I don't know,' said Porcine, who hadn't thought about that.

'Why don't I tell your father what you've done?' suggested Einstyn.

'No,' said Porcine. 'Please don't. He doesn't believe in extra-terrestrials. And he'll be so cross with me.

And anyway I promised the extra-terrestrial I wouldn't tell anyone but you.'

'I'll send you home in one of the observatory cars, then,' said Einstyn. 'You can get out at your sty and slip inside. No-one will know you were here at all.'

'That would be wonderful,' said Porcine.

'Come out the back way,' said Einstyn. He patted her hide. 'You've done very well,' he said. 'And don't worry, I won't breathe a word of this to your father. Let's hope this extra-terrestrial can succeed where science has failed.'

Chapter 14

Porcellus flew farther out into space. At any minute he expected to see the rocket heading for him. If only Porcine could persuade them not to launch it. The space stytion was coming nearer and he stared hard for any sign of the Ozosaurus.

'If I can just get near enough to the satellite to head it away from Earth, Professor Einstyn might have time to find a solution,' he thought.

He came closer and closer to the spacecraft. One of the astroporcs suddenly spotted him. Porcellus raised a trotter. 'I'm coming to help you,' he mouthed. And just at that moment, the stars around the satellite went out. The astroporcs were pressed to the port-holes, watching.

'But they can't see the Ozosaurus either,' thought Porcellus. He peered at the dark area and made out a dim shape moving towards him. A tremendous roar echoed across the sky. At the spacecraft windows, he saw the astroporcs draw back in fright.

One of the monster's feelers came snaking towards him. He dodged out of the way and the feeler curled from side to side but missed him each time. It was searching for him. Porcellus suddenly realised that, because of his stars, the Ozosaurus couldn't see where he was in the sky. If he stopped flying in a straight line and dodged about, he would be camouflaged among all the pinpoints of light.

'Where are you?' roared the monster.

'Here,' shouted Porcellus, dodging left, then right, then up, then down. 'Come and get me!'

'I'll tear you to shreds,' screamed the Ozosaurus. 'Get out and leave that satellite to me.'

'Never!' called Porcellus, zigzagging across the sky.

'I'll destroy you! I'll smash the satellite to pieces,' cried the monster. Porcellus thought quickly. Now was the time to try Porcine's plan.

'I don't believe you,' he shouted. 'You can't even catch me. I think you're feeble: I'm stronger than you.'

Something whistled past his hide and he swooped aside just in time to avoid the monster's feeler. Another huge sticky feeler curled past his snout.' 'I'll have to keep moving about,' he thought. He flew towards a cluster of stars where he could be concealed. Suddenly the stars went dark: the Ozosaurus was over there. 'I've got to lure it towards the satellite,' Porcellus decided. 'The light reflecting off the spacecraft will help me see the monster better.'

He made a quick dive back to the space stytion.

'I see you,' shrieked the Ozosaurus, throwing three of its feelers at him.

'Now,' said Porcellus to himself.

He could see the astroporcs at the portholes as he spun under the craft and up the other side. A clutching feeler unrolled towards him. Porcellus grabbed it by its smooth upper surface and threw it with all his strength back towards the Ozosaurus. It whipped across the monster's body and stuck fast against it. The Ozosaurus gave a hideous cry and lashed out at him with its other feelers but Porcellus was too quick for it. One by one, he seized the feelers and flung them back towards the monster's body until it was completely wrapped round itself in a ball. Then he zoomed towards the Ozosaurus and, summoning up his super-strength, flung it far out into deepest space. As it sped away, it gave a final scream, then burnt up like a meteorite as it flashed through the sky.

Porcellus's heart was racing and his trotters trembled. He glided slowly for a few moments to recover his strength then looked towards the satellite.

'It *was* a flying pig,' he saw the astrosow saying. 'I saw it.'

'I saw it too but it can't have been,' said the astrohog.

Porcellus flew alongside the craft. 'Look,' cried the astrosow. 'There it is again.'

'Keep calm,' called Porcellus in his loudest voice. 'Professor Einstyn's doing all he can to save you.'

He dived again below the spacecraft and tried to haul it back and slow it down by pulling on the tail-fin with his mighty strength. For a few seconds he succeeded but the speed of the space stytion was too great and he was forced to let go. He had told the astroporcs Professor Einstyn was trying to save them but he had had no word on the radio from Porcine. The astroporcs had only another three hours to go before their spacecraft re-entered Earth's gravity field and another half hour after that before they were smashed to pieces as it collided with Piggsville.

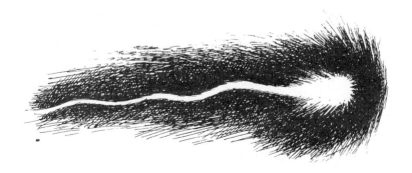

Chapter 15

'You're back early,' said Hogmanay as QMP trotted into the sty.

'I don't understand what Alboart's up to,' grunted QMP. 'I drove all the way over the observatory and when I got there, he'd decided not to launch the rocket after all. Total waste of my time.'

'But why isn't he launching it?' asked Hogmanay.

'Goodness knows,' said QMP. 'Some ridiculous idea about the U.F.O. helping the satellite or something.'

'Alboart's a very clever pig,' said his wife. 'You're always saying so yourself. Perhaps he's right.'

'A U.F.O. helpful?' said QMP. 'I think he's gone a bit crazy. Too much time spent peering through a telescope.'

Hogmanay snorted quietly. 'You spend quite a bit of time doing that yourself, QMP,' she said.

'Mine's a smaller telescope,' said QMP hastily. 'What about a nice cup of skimmed milk, my dear?'

'You'll have to get it yourself,' said Hogmanay. 'I want to put the litter to bed now.'

She got up.

The telephone rang and she picked it up. 'Why, hello, Alboart,' she said. 'Yes. Yes. Of course. Yes. QMP told me you'd changed your mind. Very wise to wait until you're sure.'

QMP moved towards the telephone but Hogmanay shook her head.

'It's Porcine he wants to speak to,' she said.

'*Porcine*,' said QMP. 'Don't be ridiculous.'

'Yes,' said Hogmanay into the telephone. 'Certainly, Alboart. I'll get her right away.'

'But why on earth does he want to speak to Porcine?' asked QMP.

'He wouldn't say,' said Hogmanay. 'Go and call her quickly, my dear. He's waiting.'

'Yes,' said Porcine into the telephone. 'I think I can. In fact I'm sure I can. Yes. It probably will. I'll do that. I think it's a very good idea too. And I'll pass it on right away. No, it's no trouble at all. I'm glad to help. All right, Professor Einstyn. Goodbye.'

She put down the telephone.

'And what was *that* about?' said QMP.

Porcine looked mysterious. 'I'm sorry but I can't tell you,' she said. 'It's top secret. And Professor Einstyn asked me to promise not to breathe a word to anyone.'

'That's RIDICULOUS!' bellowed QMP. 'I'm your *father*. Of course I should know. You tell me right this minute.'

'It's private,' said Porcine calmly. 'And secret. And I'm sorry, Father, but I can't.'

'Quite right, too,' said Hogmanay. 'Stop it, QMP. You wouldn't want a piglette who couldn't keep a secret. She's promised and it's private and that's all there is to it.'

'Humph,' grunted QMP.

'Thank you, Mother,' said Porcine. And she gave Hogmanay a hug and slipped out of the living-pen.

Chapter 16

Porcellus's radio crackled. 'Are you there? Are you all right?' came Porcine's voice.

'Your plan worked,' panted Porcellus, 'and the Ozosaurus is destroyed. But I still can't manage to stop the spacecraft. I've tried but it's going too fast and it's too heavy.'

'An amazing thing's happened,' said Porcine. 'Professor Einstyn's just telephoned me.'

'Einstyn?' said Porcellus. 'At the sty?'

'Yes,' said Porcine. 'He asked if I could contact the extra-terrestrial again. That's you, he means. And when I said I thought I could he asked me to give you an urgent message.'

'Has he got a plan to help the astroporcs?'

'No,' said Porcine. 'He says there's nothing he can do. Everything depends on the Flying Pig now. And there's only two hours to go before the space stytion's due to crash. What can you do?'

'I don't know,' said Porcellus.

'You can't just let them die,' said Porcine. 'You'll have to try to think of something. And here's Einstyn's message. He wants to know if you can manage to change the direction of the space stytion. If it heads for the sea and it can be slowed down slightly, no pigs on the ground will be killed and there's a good chance the astroporcs can be saved. The satellite was designed to land in the water so if you can possibly move it . . .'

Porcellus looked below him. It was not so dark now and he could faintly make out the outlines of the oceans. 'I'll try,' he said to Porcine. 'But I don't hold out much hope. The space stytion's just too heavy and too fast for me to move. Can't they launch a rocket to blast it into position above the sea?'

'It's too dangerous,' said Porcine. 'It might make things worse. Look out, I have to go. Mother's coming. I'll try and call you back but don't call me. I'm having awful trouble finding somewhere where no-one else can hear us. Goodbye. Good luck.'

'Goodbye,' said Porcellus. He flexed his muscles, breathed in deeply several times and flew towards the space stytion.

Chapter 17

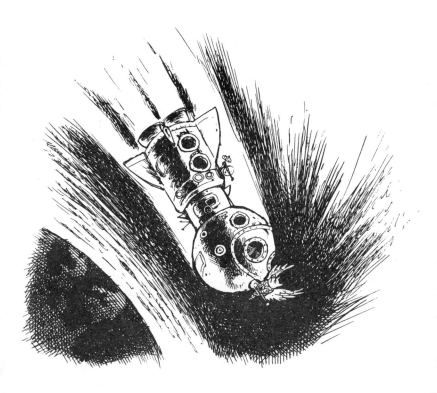

The space stytion seemed to have changed orbit once again and was now rolling over and over as it hurtled to Earth. Porcellus saw to his dismay that it was again heading directly towards Piggsville and the observatory. In a short time, the spacecraft would enter the field of Earth's gravity which would pull it downwards even faster. Seizing its tail-fin, he pulled it backwards again as hard as he could. The machine slowed slightly but he was simply not strong enough to stop it. He clutched at the nose of the craft and flapped his wings furiously but still the stricken space stytion sped on towards Earth.

'If I can't even pull it back,' thought Porcellus, 'how can I manage to guide it over the ocean?'

He tried to lock his arms around the craft and tug it sideways but his wings lacked the power to move it. 'I must stay clear of the booster rockets,' he thought. 'Even the Flying Pig isn't fireproof.' He flew above the spaceship and took a look at the radar transmission equipment, then swept past the portholes. 'I'm still trying to help you,' he called through the glass to the astroporcs. The spacepigs raised their trotters in greeting.

'I've got to save them,' Porcellus said to himself. But he couldn't think how. The space stytion began to accelerate: it had entered the field of Earth's gravity. Below them, the observatory telescope was now visible. Porcellus calculated he had about forty-five minutes left before the astroporcs crashed onto Piggsville. He examined the craft again trying to remember what Professor Einstyn had said about it. It was in two sections. The astroporcs were going to leave the control section behind and return in the front section. So the space stytion had been designed to break in two. He could even see the joint between the two pieces. If only he could pull them apart, he might be strong enough to control the two sections separately.

His radio crackled. 'It's me again,' came Porcine's voice. 'What's happening? The satellite's still coming towards us.'

'I've got one last chance,' said Porcellus. 'What I'm going to do mightn't work but it's the astroporcs' only hope. And I need every minute if I'm going to succeed. Listen, Porcine. Phone Professor Einstyn and ask him to have a rescue craft standing by in the ocean in forty minutes. Tell him I'm doing everything I possibly can to save them. OK?'

'OK,' said Porcine. 'Good luck. Over and out.'

Porcellus spat on his trotters to strengthen them, drew in a huge breath and launched himself at the space stytion. With immense force, he gripped the section break on the craft and twisted one side to the west and the other to the east. For a moment the metal resisted, then it slowly began to break apart. Porcellus tugged hard on the front section and the space stytion split in two. Through the front portholes, he saw the astroporcs cheering.

Hauling the smaller, lighter back section, he flew towards a large chain of deserted mountains. Positioning himself above their snowy peaks, he flung the rear of the spacecraft straight down into their midst where it could crash harmlessly. Then he raced over to the satellite and pulled backwards on its fin until he felt it gradually slow down.

'Twenty-five minutes to go,' he thought. 'But we're right over Piggsville. Even if I slow the satellite, it will still smash the astroporcs and the city below when it crashes. And I'm starting to get tired. I can't keep on holding it back much longer.' He could see the ocean clearly, away to his left. 'It's getting lighter,' he said aloud. 'It must be about five o'clock in the morning now.'

With so little time left, there was only one way he could move the satellite over the ocean. He would have to ram it with his body.

Dropping the fin, he flew swiftly away, lined himself up with the side of the craft and swooshed straight at it with his trotters outstretched. As they made contact with the side, he summoned up all his mighty strength and pushed as hard as he could. The nose of the satellite swung sideways and the capsule began to head down towards the sea. Using his super-sight, Porcellus scanned the ocean and made out a rescue boat just setting out.

Ten minutes to go now. The satellite was gathering speed again. Porcellus hauled hard on the fin pulling the craft back, farther back, even farther back, until – with five minutes to go – it slowed to a gentle glide and hovered half a mile above the surface of the ocean. In the rescue boat, Porcellus could make out Professor Einstyn anxiously watching and on the beach he could see crowds of porkers gathering for the splash-down.

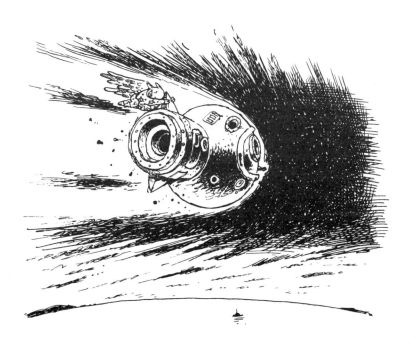

He made a decision. Now was the moment to let the satellite drop down into the sea. Carefully, he let go of the fin, pushed the nose forward, hauled back briefly on the fin again and watched as the spacecraft glided to Earth. As its nose touched the ocean, it slipped forward and settled safely on the surface of the water and two plastic floats came sliding out from a compartment under the belly.

The crowd bellowed and roared. Porcellus could see Einstyn shouting congratulations and the astroporcs cheering through the portholes. The sun was just beginning to show over the horizon. 'I must get back to the sty before anyone notices I'm missing,' he thought. And with the jubilant cheers of the crowd in his ears, he flew unnoticed back towards Piggsville.

Chapter 18

Porcellus landed behind the garage and waited for his stars to fade and his wings to shrink. They didn't. 'I can't go indoors like this,' he thought. 'I'll have to wait out here until I'm normal again.' There was a light in the living-pen so he crept to the window and peered through. The whole family was sitting in night-clothes staring at the television set where the astrosow was climbing out of the satellite into the rescue boat and shaking trotters with Professor Einstyn. In a nearby boat, reporters were shouting questions.

'I'm from *The Gruntchester News*. What happened?' shouted one.

'I'm from *The Stymes*. How did you land the satellite?' cried another.

'Please make a statement to the *Ham and Sty*,' called a third.

'No statements,' said Einstyn firmly as the astrohog clambered out and waved to the television cameras. 'It was a Flying Pig,' he said, looking dazed. 'I saw it myself. Gold with multi-coloured wings. We wouldn't be alive now if . . .'

'No statements yet,' said Einstyn hastily, helping him into the boat, 'De-briefing first, some rest next and then the press conference can start.'

Porcellus pressed his snout against the glass watching the television commentators and the crowds lining the beach waiting for the astroporcs. Suddenly, Hogmanay got up and began counting heads. 'Eleven, twelve, thirteen . . .' She turned to her husband. 'One of the litter's missing, my dear.' Porcellus shrank down out of sight. 'It's Porcellus,' she said. 'He must be still asleep. I'll go and fetch him.'

'Quickly,' said QMP. 'It's an historic moment. He

mustn't miss it.'

Porcine leapt to her trotters. 'I'll go, Mother,' she cried. 'You stay and watch the television.'

'What a thoughtful little piglette you are,' said Hogmanay.

Porcine disappeared and Porcellus crept round to the bed-pen window. Just as he was about to tap on the glass he felt his wings quiver and wobble. He looked down as his chest: his stars were disappearing as he watched. 'Porcine,' he whispered, 'I'm out here. Quick.'

She opened the window and helped him to scramble in. 'I couldn't come in before,' he said. 'I was still the Flying Pig.'

'Here. Climb into your night clothes,' said Porcine. 'Hurry!'

As Porcellus hauled on his pyjamas, she went to the door. 'He's just coming,' she called.

'But what about Mother and Father?' said Porcellus. 'Einstyn phoned you here. Do they know what it was about?'

'Not a clue,' said Porcine. 'I refused to utter a grunt. Father was furious. And Einstyn doesn't know the U.F.O. was you either. He just knows I was in contact with it.' She ruffled Porcellus's hide. 'Yawn,' she said. 'Try to look sleepy.'

'I *am* sleepy,' said Porcellus.

Porcine kissed his snout. 'You were wonderful,' she said.

'So were you,' said Porcellus as they went out into the living-pen together.

'*Porcellus*,' said his father. 'I don't believe it. You've slept through all the excitement. The astroporcs are safe. We've been watching the landing on television but I'm afraid you've missed the best part.'

'I don't mind,' said Porcellus, giving a huge yawn.

'Here,' said his mother. 'A nice mug of acorn soup.'

He took a sip of his soup as he watched Professor Einstyn help the astroporcs through the cheering crowds. He yawned again.

'I can't think why you're so tired,' said his mother. 'You'd better sleep in in the morning.'

Porcine winked at Porcellus. He winked back.

'All right, Mother,' he said. 'I think I will.'